Papa's Latkes

Michelle Edwards

illustrated by Stacey Schuett

CANDLEWICK PRESS
CAMBRIDGE, MASSACHUSETTS

First edition 2004

Library of Congress Cataloging-in-Publication Data
Edwards, Michelle.
Papa's latkes / Michelle Edwards ; illustrated by Stacey Schuett. —1st ed.
p. cm.
Summary: On the first Hanukkah after Mama died,
Papa and his two daughters try to make latkes and celebrate without her.
ISBN 0-7636-0779-7
[1. Hanukkah—Fiction. 2. Single-parent families—Fiction.
3. Fathers—Fiction. 4. Jews—United States—Fiction.]
I. Schuett, Stacey, ill. II. Title.
PZ7.E262 Pap 2001
[E]—dc21   00-069801

2 4 6 8 10 9 7 5 3 1

Printed in China

This book was typeset in Stempel Schneidler.
The illustrations were done in oil with acrylic gouache.

Candlewick Press
2067 Massachusetts Avenue
Cambridge, Massachusetts 02140

visit us at www.candlewick.com

To children young and old
who miss their mothers at Chanukah
M. E.

In memory of my mother, Rita Kimball
S. S.

Selma and her little sister, Dora, were waiting for Papa to come home. It was their first Chanukah without Mama. Selma's heart ached when she remembered how sick and thin Mama had looked last summer. Thin enough to be blown away by a light summer breeze. And then, right before school started, Mama died.

Selma polished Great-Grandma Skolnick's silver menorah.
How she wished Mama could see how brightly it gleamed.
Mama could inspect the menorah from top to bottom.
This year Selma hadn't missed a spot.

"Put the menorah on the table by the window so later
the whole neighborhood will see how brightly our candles
burn," Selma told Dora. It was exactly what Mama had
always told Selma.

"I hear footsteps," Dora said. Selma heard them, too.

"Ho, ho, ho," a loud voice rang from the stairwell.

"Santa Claus?" called out Dora. Selma smiled at her little sister.

"Santa Claus, Shmanta Claus! Whoever heard of a Jewish Santa Claus carrying a fifty-pound bag of potatoes?"

It was Papa. Selma ran to help him.

"Ho, ho, ho! Oy, oy, oy! Is this ever heavy!" said Papa.

Papa gave Selma and Dora each a small grocery
sack and put the big bag of potatoes on the floor.

"For the first night of Chanukah, my good
friend Smuelkoff from the corner grocery
store has loaded me up with everything
we need to make latkes," he announced.

"We have potatoes enough for the Russian
and American armed forces," continued
Papa. "Oil for a hundred and twenty
nights, and onions enough to keep you
crying till Passover. Also we have sour
cream, applesauce, jam, and matzo meal."

"Nu, let's make latkes," said Papa.
He clapped his hands together.

"We don't know how," said Dora.
"Mama always made them."

Selma smiled. Mama was like an army
sergeant in the kitchen on Chanukah.
She would have everything ready to begin
before Selma even came home from school.
Could they just open the packages and
start cooking? Could they make latkes
without her?

Selma had been Mama's second-in-command in the kitchen every Chanukah. She had to remember what Mama had taught her.

"I'd scrub the potatoes. Mama would peel the onions and grate them with the potatoes. First a potato, then an onion," Selma told Papa. "I'll scrub the potatoes and you peel the onions."

"All right," he said. "I will grate potato, onion, potato, onion, potato, onion, cha, cha, cha."

"I helped Mama, too," added Dora. "I cracked the eggs, and I know how to beat them with a fork."

"Ta-da! Eggs for Miss Dora Skolnick, champion egg beater." Papa gave Dora a bowl, a fork, and six eggs.

Selma grabbed an apron. She thought some more.

"We can't forget the matzo meal. Mama always added a handful before she mixed the batter. It helps keep them together," said Selma, remembering Mama's big hands, dusty with matzo meal.

So they began. The kitchen hummed with work. Soon the big green bowl was filled with grated potatoes and onions, eggs, and matzo meal.

"I'm hungry," said Dora.

"Latke time," said Papa. "What do we do next?"

"You have to fry them," said Selma. "Mama always did that part all by herself." Mama didn't want Selma and Dora near the pan with bubbling-hot oil. Selma had to sit at the kitchen table and read to Dora.

"I'll fry them," said Papa. "How hard could it be?"
He got out Mama's big black pan and poured oil into it.

"Can't be stingy with oil on Chanukah," said Papa.
He poured the rest of the oil in the bottle into the pan
and turned on the stove. Selma watched him sing while
he slapped down the potato batter and fried the first latkes.
She remembered Mama by the stove last Chanukah, before
she got sick. Her hair was like a halo around her face,
her cheeks pink from the heat.

The apartment smelled like potatoes and onions. The air was rich with that Chanukah smell. Dora stood by the stove, singing with Papa. Selma set the table with the tablecloth and napkins that Mama had embroidered with menorahs and dreidels and stars of David. She put the applesauce and jam and sour cream into the green glass bowls that Grandma Yetta had carried with her from Poland. She found the good silver forks and put them next to the blue holiday plates.

Three plates, Selma reminded herself. Just three
plates this Chanukah. She had left the blue plate with
the little white chip in the breakfront, the plate Mama
always insisted on using for herself.

"Latkes!" announced Papa in a big, happy voice. "Poetry on a platter!"

He brought the latkes to the table. Mama's latkes were always golden brown and light and crisp. Selma thought Papa's latkes looked like the mud pies she and Dora made in the summer. They were fat and brown and lumpy.

"So, let's eat," said Papa. He put mountains of sour cream on his lumpy latkes.

"Delicious," said Papa, patting his stomach.

Dora smeared jam all over her latkes and made latke sandwiches.

"Yum," she said.

Selma took a tiny spoonful of applesauce and put it on her big, fat, brown, lumpy latke. But she couldn't eat. Papa's latkes shouldn't look like this. They should look like Mama's latkes. Chanukah shouldn't be like this. Three people in the kitchen instead of four. Chanukah should be like it always was, with Mama. Then she began to cry.

"You feel sick?" asked Papa.

Selma shook her head.

"The latkes?" asked Papa.

Selma cried harder. She couldn't speak.

"Your latkes were good. I liked them," Dora explained. Then she looked at Selma. "But they weren't like Mama's."

"You are right," said Papa. "Papa's latkes are like Papa, a little too heavy maybe around the middle." Papa rubbed his stomach. He laughed a little laugh.

Selma had always laughed when Papa made jokes about his big belly, but tonight Selma couldn't.

"Selma," said Papa softly, "Mama isn't here, but we are. We can remember Mama. And we can make latkes, and we can still celebrate Chanukah. That is what Mama would want us to do."

Selma walked over and hugged Papa.

"Hey, me too," said Dora.

Selma opened her arms, and Dora ran over and joined in the hug. They hugged like that for a long time, Selma and Papa and Dora. A Skolnick family hug.

The room grew darker, and Selma could see the stars outside their window.

"Papa, may I light the candles tonight?'" asked Selma.

"Of course," said Papa.

Papa said the prayers while Selma lit the candles the way Mama had taught her. First the shammes and then, with the shammes, she lit the first candle of Chanukah. Dora sang "Rock of Ages" from beginning to end, all by herself.

"Happy Chanukah," said Selma.

"Happy Chanukah," said Papa and Dora.
And in the quiet room, Selma whispered,
"Happy Chanukah, Mama."